Trouble on Tatooine
NOVEL

STAR WARS® ADVENTURES

Trouble on Tatooine

Dave Wolverton

LUCAS BOOKS

SCHOLASTIC INC.

New York • Toronto • London • Auckland • Sydney
Mexico City • New Delhi • Hong Kong • Buenos Aires

ISBN 0-439-45889-7

12 11 10 9 8 7 6 5 4 3 2 1.   3 4 5 6 7 8/0

Printed in the U.S.A.
First Scholastic printing, April 2000

Trouble on Tatooine

CHAPTER ONE

Kitster was dreaming again. In his dream, he was a little boy, sitting on his father's lap. They were on a spaceship, on a bridge, and his father was holding him tightly as they blasted into hyperspace.

He couldn't remember what his father's face looked like. His father was a big man, with dark hair. But in the dream, Kitster vividly saw his father's right hand. Kitster traced a ragged white scar that ran from the joint of his father's thumb up to the middle of his wrist. His father wore a golden bracelet that looked like a slave's manacle.

Kitster was studying the bracelet when his father said, "Here we go."

Suddenly his chair began to shudder, and the outside became streaks of light as the ship quickened into hyperspace.

Kitster sat gaping, enthralled by the light show. His father hugged him. "You're going to go far in life," he said.

* * *

"On your feet, slave!" a deep voice growled. Kitster felt a sharp pain as someone kicked him in the ribs.

He woke in a daze, and found himself lying in the dirt, beneath a tall tree. It took him a moment to recall where he was and how he'd gotten here. *The escape!*

It came back in a flash. He'd brought Dorn here to Gardulla the Hutt's pleasure garden to wait with Pala

3

and the Ghostling children. They were supposed to escape from Tatooine.

Only at the last minute, Sebulba and his companions had found them. Kitster had been trying to sneak out when he'd been hit by a STUN blast.

Now he was awake. He crawled to his hands and knees, but couldn't get up. His ears were ringing. He felt so dizzy he couldn't stand. Metal cuffs bound his wrists.

"You heard me. On your feet!" Kitster's captor yanked a chain. The binders on his hands snapped forward. He fell with a groan.

Captured. I've been captured. His stomach tightened as he swallowed his panic. He'd tried to free the Ghostling children, so they could go home to their parents. But the law on Tatooine forbade anyone from helping slaves escape. There was only one punishment for what he'd done—death.

Kitster hoped that his friends had gotten away. He thought of Anakin, Pala, Dorn, Princess Arawynne, and the other Ghostling children. If they escaped, he'd be happy.

"Up, I say!" Another boot slammed into Kitster. He steeled himself for the ordeal ahead. He climbed to his knees, and made it to his feet.

He had no idea how long he'd been knocked out. He felt surprised to see that it was still daytime. He judged by the shadows that it was still a couple of hours until sundown.

His guard was a Weequay, who held the chains that bound Kitster in a beefy brown fist. Kitster pulled back, and the guard gave him a hard tug. The force of it yanked Kitster off his feet.

Kitster felt too weak to fight, or even to walk on his own. His wrists hurt horribly. The Weequay didn't mind if Kitster couldn't walk. He simply pulled the chain, dragging Kitster down the bumpy trail.

The guard didn't drag him far. The Weequay took him to the door of the pleasure garden and let Kitster lie. Several more Weequay stood watch there. Kitster groaned.

Dorn lay on the ground nearby. He was still knocked out.

"We've caught the Ghostlings and the pesky little Twi'lek," someone said over a guard's comlink. It took Kitster a moment to recognize Sebulba's voice. "I think there may be one more kid hiding in here. I saw three kids dressed up in Jawas' robes. So keep your eyes open."

Kitster's heart pounded. The kid had to be Anakin. He hoped with all his might that his best friend would escape.

The guard standing above Kitster received one more message on his com

"Transport the prisoners to the holding pens at the arena," Sebulba instructed.

Kitster and his friends were trapped!

CHAPTER TWO

Jira stood in the hot Tatooine air, a blue rag tied around her stringy gray hair, squinting at passersby and calling, "Fruit. Get your fruit here." The small canopy over her stand didn't provide enough shade for her to stand in.

Jawas, moisture farmers, and creatures from a hundred worlds passed her by. They headed for the cool, dark cantinas, sheltered from Tatooine's twin suns.

Anakin ran up to her rickety stand.

"Hello, Annie," Jira said loudly. "What can I do for you?"

Anakin tried to hide the desperation in his voice as he whispered, "I need help. Pala and Dorn and Kitster have all been captured with the Ghostling children!"

Jira's breath caught in her throat, and she gave a little cough of surprise. She glanced around, as if searching for a place to sit. Anakin could see the hope and joy go out of her eyes, as if he'd just struck her.

"Oh," she said loudly, for any passerby who might be listening. "You want something special. I think I have one back home."

She closed her little fruit stand, and Anakin followed her through the dusty streets, toward her quarters. They rounded a droid who was cleaning up after a dewback, then passed a couple of beefy

Baragwins who were wrestling in the street while people made bets on the outcome.

As they strode purposefully along, a loudspeaker set atop a nearby vaporator tower announced, "There will be a slave execution at sunset tonight, in the arena. The public is invited to attend. Reserve your seat now—only five wupiupi!"

Anakin tried not to reveal the depth of his fear. He knew what was happening.

They reached Jira's small quarters. Anakin was again shocked at how barren it was.

As soon as the door closed, Jira turned with a sad expression. "Annie, you're a good boy."

Anakin nodded. He could tell that she had bad news.

"You and your friends tried to do what was right," Jira said. "And for that, your friends might have to pay with their lives."

"I don't want to hear this," Anakin said.

"You have to hear it. There's a ship coming tonight, in less than four hours. It was supposed to take the Ghostling children away. Now I think that you should go, instead."

"No!" Anakin said. He couldn't bear the thought of leaving his friends to die.

"I'm telling you this for your own good. There's nothing left that you can do."

"You're the one who told us to have hope," Anakin said. "You're the one who said that there's always hope."

Jira shook her head sadly. "I didn't get the money," she admitted. "I got part of it, but not nearly enough. Maybe if we give them the money I've got, the smugglers will take you away, instead."

Anakin looked at her fiercely. His eyes felt as if they were burning, and he fought back tears. "Get the money," he said. "Any way you can. And be ready at sunset. I'll be ready. And so will my friends."

CHAPTER THREE

Kitster lay in the dirt beside Dorn at the door to the pleasure garden. His wrists were so swollen that the irons felt as if they were shrinking, getting tighter with each passing minute.

He kept thinking about escape. He had spent most of his life thinking about escape, but this time he was even more desperate. He watched the guards, hoping that they would turn their backs.

If I can escape, he wondered, *where do I go?*

So far, no one had recognized him. He'd kept his face mostly covered by the reddish-brown Jawa robe. But Gardulla the Hutt owned Kitster. Sooner or later, someone in the fortress would recognize him.

Then there would be no escape. Once they knew his name, all they had to do was push the button on his transmitter and...

The handcuffs themselves gave Kitster an idea. They were black with grease.

Kitster's face was dark. By scraping some of the black grease off the irons and rubbing it on his face and hands, he managed to make himself even darker. He didn't get as black as a Sakiyan, but it was close.

There was no disguising Dorn. His pelt and his enormous long eyebrows marked him as a Bothan. The slave masters already knew his name.

Kitster lay on the grass. Big trees rose up nearby, with vines and moss hanging from them. Someone had turned the waterfall back on, so that it tumbled from rocks on the hillside, but it was only a soft rumble.

Soon, Djas Puhr and some other guards brought in Pala and the Ghostling children. They were chained together at their feet so that no one could run.

Pala walked in the lead with her head down. Her twin head-tails hung limply down her back. Princess Arawynne followed behind her, breathing hard. The other children trailed along quietly. They didn't seem to be too afraid. That was good. They didn't know what Sebulba had planned for them.

Djas Puhr made them stop, then snapped a manacle onto Kitster's foot and chained him to Pala, so that he would be in the lead.

Kitster felt his stomach tighten in terror. Now that he was locked to the others, escape seemed even less likely.

When Djas Puhr finished, he chained Dorn to the last child in line.

Gardulla the Hutt pushed into the garden. She heaved her enormous body through the door and looked at the children all locked together.

"Ah, such a pity," Gardulla said. "Such a waste of good slaves!"

At that, the Ghostling children's eyes all went wide. Some of them began pulling on their chains, each wanting to run in a different direction. Others just stood and cried.

"Oh, Great One," Pala begged. Gardulla turned her huge golden eyes on the young Twi'lek girl. "Please, let the Ghostlings go. It wasn't their idea to break out. It was mine. I'm the one at fault here!"

Gardulla smiled broadly. "That's so *noble* of you, offering to sacrifice yourself for them. But you *all* escaped. You bombed my fortress, blew up my droids, burned me with Podracer exhaust, and squirted some really nasty cleanser in my mouth. I really must make an example of you all, don't you think? If I don't, people will say I'm going soft."

"Please," Pala repeated. "They're just children. Let them live as your slaves, and you'll have them a good long time."

Gardulla laughed at the idea. "You tempt me. They *are* pretty," she said. "I'll tell you what, I'll make you a bargain. One of your friends has escaped. Tell me his name, and I'll give you the lives of *two* Ghostling children in exchange."

Pala stepped backward. She glanced around in terror.

Kitster wondered: *Would she really give up Anakin's life in exchange for two children she barely knew?*

She said nothing.

"As I thought," Gardulla said.

Gardulla slithered closer, and examined Dorn. "Jabba had such great hopes for you."

She reached up to Dorn's neck and touched the tiny signal jammer that Anakin had made for him. It looked like a plain old necklace that a slave might wear. She held it up, letting it dangle in the light. "Ingenious," Gardulla said. "A real work of art."

She drew close to Kitster. He stood with his hands clasped, looking at the ground. The hood of his robe covered his face.

"Look at me," Gardulla ordered.

Kitster looked up and held his breath. Gardulla had lots of slaves, thousands of them. Would she recognize him? She took one glance at his dark, dark face. No hint of recognition showed in her eyes. "What of you, little one? Life is so precious, don't you think? What if I offer you your life, in exchange for your friend's?"

He knew that she was lying. She'd never keep such a bargain. "What kind of friend would I be, if I did that?"

"A smart friend," Gardulla said. "A living friend."

Kitster heard a pulsing noise. He recognized it immediately. It was the sound of an interrogator droid.

He glanced at the garden door and saw the droid, like a round globe, come gliding through. Its red electronic eye scanned the group. The children behind Kitster began to whimper and back away. They fought against their chains.

"Well, since you're first in line," Gardulla said to Kitster, "I'll give you first chance to talk."

The droid swept forward on its repulsorlift engine. Kitster prepared for his first interrogation.

CHAPTER FOUR

Anakin wasn't going to just *talk* about having hope. He was going to act on it.

The first thing he had to do was to figure out how to save his friends. He thought about where Kitster and the others were being taken—the Mos Espa Arena.

The arena was where they held Podraces, but sometimes the Hutts sponsored fights there, too. Since the fights were between some of the most fearsome creatures in the galaxy, the arena had some holding pens built where beasts could be locked away until they fought.

That's where they'd keep Anakin's friends and the Ghostling children, in some pen built for monsters. The problem was, those pens were designed for huge, cruel beings—not kids.

Anakin considered how to get his friends out. He couldn't hope to disarm the guards. Nor could he overpower them or trick them.

No, the best way to get his friends out would be to sneak them out. But it wouldn't be easy.

He could think of only one entrance that might lead to the holding pens: The sand drains.

There were some pretty big drainage pipes running under the city, taking extra sand from the buildings. With luck, the pipes would be big enough to crawl through.

He ran home, and went to his room. It was the middle of the day, and Watto would be waiting for him to get back from his errands.

Anakin knew he'd have to stall. If he managed to get his friends free, he could tell Watto the errands had taken him much longer than they actually had. The Toydarian would be mad, and he'd make Anakin work overtime for days, just to teach him a lesson. But Anakin's friends were worth the risk.

Anakin checked through the stuff in his room. There was lots of old junk in his cubbyholes: model spaceships, parts to old droids. Some of the junk was worth money. But none of it, except maybe his Jawa ion blaster, would help him get his friends free.

Anakin swept the valuable stuff into a big bag, and then lugged it down to the market. He quickly sold his stuff to a dealer. Then he bought what he needed—glow rods, sandmasks, and a hand-held beamdrill. When he finished, he didn't have any money left over.

By then, more than an hour had passed. There was still no sign of Gardulla the Hutt and the kids.

This made it easier for Anakin to break into the holding pens. He simply walked into the unguarded arena. There he found a large drain that carried sand out when the cleaning droids swept the floors. Anakin unfastened the grill over the drain and began to explore the pipes beneath the arena.

CHAPTER FIVE

"This isn't working," Sebulba complained as the interrogator droid circled Pala again.

The Twi'lek girl stood mutely. She clenched her teeth, and her head-tails lashed, but she did not want to show any sign of discomfort. Still, there was a haunted look in her eyes that suggested she could be broken.

"Tell us what we want to know," Gardulla demanded, "and the pain will stop. Who helped you escape?"

"No one!" Pala said for the twentieth time.

The interrogator droid whined in her ears. Pala cringed, but did not try to escape the shrill noise. "Maybe you should turn up the volume," Pala suggested. "Madame Vansitt can yell louder than this."

Sebulba was outraged.

He'd captured the children nearly three hours ago, and the interrogator droid had failed to break both Kitster and Pala. "She's as bad as the boy," he grumbled. "None of these children will talk. They know they only have to hold out for a little while longer."

Gardulla glanced at a wall chrono. The executions were scheduled in just over an hour. She didn't have time to torture the children anymore.

"Very well, then," she said. "Let them take their secret to the grave. If they want to protect their friend, it doesn't matter."

"Doesn't matter?" Sebulba asked, livid.

"He's just one more child," Gardulla said. "What can one child do?"

With that, she waved her hand. The guards came forward and escorted the children to a transport.

In moments they would be on their way to the Mos Espa Arena, to meet their fates.

The transport crawled over the sandy road to Mos Espa. It wound through canyons of red rock, where the wild Sand People once raised their hubba gourds in abundance, and took shelter from the fierce desert storms.

The transport came bouncing over the uneven streets of the city. Onlookers stopped to gaze through the transparisteel windows.

The suns were falling, bringing the last dusk that Dorn would ever see.

Dorn stared out at curious droids, their eyes bright. Jawas lined the streets. Free creatures—like Gardulla's henchmen or criminals from the space station—shook their fists and jeered at the children. One Rodian threw a dirt clod. Fellow slaves looked through the glass with resignation, sympathy, or abject terror.

Dorn felt as if he were a freak, some gloriously strange creature from offworld who had caught everyone's attention.

It's my fault, he thought. *I could have saved my friends. All I had to do was stay away from them, and none of them would have been caught.*

Worse than that, it had been Dorn's idea to try to save the Ghostling children in the first place. He'd dared Anakin and Kitster to come with him.

I could have left things alone, he thought. *I could have let the Ghostlings live as slaves. At least they would have lived.*

All around him, the Ghostling children sat in chains, weeping. They were beautiful creatures, flawless. Each had a strange light that glowed from within them.

Some of the people of Mos Espa, upon seeing the Ghostlings headed to their death, turned away and stifled sobs of their own.

Dorn wished he could do it all over again. He wished he could find some way to take back his deeds and make everything right.

Soon he saw the arena in the distance, its lights already shining in the late afternoon. It rose above the desert on the outskirts of Mos Espa. Crowds of slaves and free people alike were filing through its gates.

Music played. A commentator announced the night's events.

The slaves entered for free. Some were required by their masters to watch what happened to any slave who dared try to escape from Tatooine.

But the free people paid for their own entrance, a minimal fee to satisfy their morbid curiosity. Gardulla would make sure that Dorn's death and the deaths of his friends were entertaining, so that the crowd would pay to watch next time.

The transport slid down to the loading docks, where dangerous monsters were normally offloaded.

Dangerous monsters—is that what they think we are? Dorn wondered.

Dorn suddenly understood that he *was* dangerous. He was dangerous because he had stood up to evil—because he had dared to say no.

In a corner of the galaxy where corrupt leaders ruled only because decent citizens did not dare to resist, that made Dorn the most dangerous kind of being around.

In minutes, the guards had the back of the transport open. With stun batons in hand, they ordered the children out.

Kitster led the way, followed by Pala and the Ghostling children. Dorn came last.

They marched to their cell, and Dorn wondered what Gardulla had planned. Would she give the Ghostling children weapons and force them to fight one another? Or did she have something more diabolical in mind?

He passed a door, and behind it heard roaring. It sounded like a Krayt dragon. That seemed to answer his question.

At last they reached a cell, and the others all filed in. But Dorn stopped at the door.

A huge Gamorrean guard stood there. He had blue blotches on his green cheeks, and oversized tusks that stuck out from his piggy jaw. His red eyes blazed at Dorn as he pushed him into the cell.

Dorn stared him in the eye. The hulking guard was afraid of him. "I defy you," Dorn said.

The guard clubbed Dorn with the stun baton. The blow itself would have knocked him down, but the electric shock added another layer of pain.

Dorn crumpled to the ground. The guard slammed the door.

No matter what, Dorn thought, *I defy you still.*

Anakin could hear the children crying, even above the clamor of announcers on the loudspeakers out in the arena, even over swelling music of the orchestra.

He followed the sound and soon found himself under a holding cell. Using his beamdrill, he'd cut the pins that held the grill to the drain an hour ago. Now he pushed his head through. Anakin saw the Ghostling children all chained together.

The iron chain ran through a ring in each child's manacle. Locks held the chain to Dorn's hand in the back, and Kitster's in the front.

Anakin climbed through with his beamdrill.

He had to hurry. It was getting dark outside, and the guards would be coming any moment. He'd hoped for more time. He needed time to free the Ghostlings, time to escape, and more time to reach Jira and her smuggler friends out in the desert.

Dorn, Kitster, and Pala looked *very* happy to see him. But there was no time to lose. The plasma beam cutting torch on the drill quickly carved through the locks.

Anakin urged everyone into the drainpipe, crawled down himself, and pulled the grate back over the pipe.

He heard the door scraping open above.

A guard shouted, "Sound the alarms!"

At this point, you must decide whether to continue reading this adventure, or to play your own adventure in the *Star Wars* Adventures Game Book, *Trouble on Tatooine*.

To play your own adventure, turn to the first page of the Game Book and follow the directions you find there.

To continue reading this adventure, turn the page!

CHAPTER SIX

Anakin followed Dorn and the others through the drainpipes. Sand flew everywhere. Anakin made sure that he gave each kid a sandmask, just to make it through the pipes. He didn't want anyone to choke.

He had only three glow rods. Up front, Dorn carried one. A child in the middle of the group took another, and Anakin held the last. All hc could see were jumbled shadows and the feet and legs of the Ghostling boy that crawled directly ahead of him.

The pipes were hardly big enough for a child to squeeze through. Anakin had to wriggle through the flowing sand, pulling himself on his elbows, pushing with his toes.

Anakin pushed the Jawa ion blaster into his sack.

"I'm at a junction," Dorn yelled after they'd crawled for some time.

Anakin took a deep breath, removed his mask, and shouted, "Head down to the right! Go till the second pipe opens overhead. That will take us to the Podrace hangar."

Distant alarms wailed, echoing spookily through the pipes. Anakin hoped that the signal jammers he'd made for his friends kept working. If they didn't someone's transmitter might give their location away.

"Watch out behind you," Pala shouted through the pipe to Anakin. "They'll be sending capture droids."

Anakin knew that.

Capture droids were made to hunt for fugitives. Like seekers, they could track by scent. Their infared eyes could see in the dark. Their stunners could knock even the biggest man down. They could crawl into tight spaces.

And once they got their claws into you, they wouldn't let go.

Right now, Anakin couldn't stop them. As long as he was stuck in this narrow pipe, he couldn't turn around to shoot his ion blaster.

"Hurry!" Anakin shouted.

The children scurried as fast as they could. Overhead, behind him, Anakin heard guards yelling, followed by the sound of the metal grate scraping against the pipes. He listened for the telltale sound of mechanical legs scrabbling at his back.

The child in front of him suddenly waded into some deeper sand. He'd reached the juncture. Three small pipes met here in a box, then the sand blew into a windpipe down below.

From behind came a scraping sound, the *rap, tap, tap* of mechanical feet scurrying through pipes.

Anakin dove headfirst down the pipe at the juncture and came up with his Jawa ion blaster. He didn't dare stick his head up where the capture droid could get him.

He simply thrust the barrel of the ion blaster into the open pipe, then fired. The blaster wouldn't damage any creatures but droids. Blue ionized gases roared through the pipe.

Three electronic vocoders squealed, echoing in the enclosed space. Anakin's mouth dropped in astonishment. There had been *three* capture droids in the pipe.

Charges of energy shot through the droids. They slumped together in a heap, useless.

The blast hurled Anakin back. He crawled forward, ears ringing.

Anakin listened for more signs of pursuit from the capture droids. He heard none. He dove into the larger pipe. It was only a hand-span wider than the one he'd just come through, but it felt much bigger.

Earlier the sand had been still. Now it swirled all around him.

It pushed him along rapidly. He followed at the feet of the child in front of him. It was a hundred meters from the Podrace hangar—or at least that's what he guessed.

He reached the juncture and saw the Ghostling child in front of him try frantically to crawl up it. But sand rushed from the pipe, creating a strong current, and Ghostlings were so frail. The Ghostling couldn't make it!

Furiously the child kicked and pushed against the side of the pipes, but the sand won, pushing him off farther into the system.

Anakin reached the pipe and tried to push himself up. Sand seethed around him. It was a torrent.

He could think of only one reason for so much sand: The slave masters were flooding the pipes! The children would be smothered.

Perhaps they were trying to kill the children, or perhaps they were only trying to cut off their escape route.

In any case, Anakin couldn't make it up the pipe. He could only follow the current of sand and the Ghostlings.

CHAPTER SEVEN

Anakin hurtled through the pipes. Sand shoved and jostled him.

He couldn't stop. He couldn't slow. He dropped his bag with the ion blaster and his beamdrill, and slid along as best he could, clinging to his glow rod.

The Ghostlings, Pala, Dorn, and Kitster all drifted ahead faster than he did. Anakin lost sight of them. He had no idea how fast he was going, or how far.

The torrent swept him for perhaps a thousand meters, past opening after opening, pipes that could have led anywhere.

Suddenly the pipe opened up, and the flood spat him into a chasm. He flew headlong into a dune.

He managed to cling to his glow rod. In the drifts below, he spotted his bag with the Jawa ion blaster and the other supplies in it. It was sinking! But his lungs were hurting. The dust was choking him.

He left the bag, stood up for fresh air, and coughed until his lungs cleared. He put the sandmask back on and dove again.

Frantically, he reached down for his bag. The currents of sand shoved the bag deeper, as if to lure him farther away from his friends.

He surfaced for breath and saw something: The trail of a monster.

He had no sooner seen the trail than the creature appeared.

A rock wart!

An orange leg wrapped around his arm, and another reached toward the glow rod. It was trying to pull the glow rod away.

Anakin wrestled with the monster, wishing that he had a weapon. But all his tools were at the bottom of the dune.

He managed to pull the sandmask from his mouth with his free hand. A clawed foot came into view.

Anakin bit the claw with all his might.

The monster shrieked. Suddenly the rock wart quit fighting to steal his glow rod and began fighting to escape.

Anakin bit it again for good measure. The wart scurried away.

Anakin ducked under the sand and grasped his tool bag. Then he stood and raised his glow rod in order to get his bearings.

The children had waded into a large chamber, perhaps eighty meters long and forty meters wide. The low ceiling was cut from stone.

Dozens of pipes opened into the chamber. It seemed to serve as some kind of catch basin, where large objects could be cleared from the drainage.

In the sand around him, Anakin could see Ghostling children. The small boy that Anakin had been following coughed. He raised his head feebly, and let the sand cover him.

Anakin grabbed the child from behind, and tried to pull him to safety.

"Over here!" Pala shouted. In the corner was a landing, a solid spot where everyone could sit.

"Get out of the sand!" Anakin warned. "There's something down here with us!"

He flailed, trying to drag the little boy with him.

The children struggled, thrashing in the sand, until they reached the landing. They launched themselves onto it and sat, coughing, as they studied the sand's surface.

Anakin got the child to safety.

"There's a monster in here?" Princess Arawynne asked. Some of the Ghostling children began to cry.

"Yeah," Anakin said. "And it tastes awful."

"What do we do if it comes after us?" one Ghostling child asked. He couldn't hide the terror in his voice.

"I bit it hard," Anakin said. "That scared it away— at least for now. You can all take a bite, if it comes back."

Anakin shoved the child onto the landing. The boy couldn't stop coughing.

Oh no, Anakin thought. *He's hurt, and I don't know how to get out of here. We're in deep trouble.*

CHAPTER EIGHT

"Someone has to find us a way out of here," Arawynne said.

Anakin felt so tired, he could barely move. But he couldn't let his friends down.

"I'll go," he offered. If anyone spotted Pala or Dorn or one of the Ghostlings, they'd be recognized as escapees instantly. Anakin had surprise on his side.

As long as nobody was looking for him.

"Hurry," Arawynne begged. "They will be after us."

Anakin nodded.

He looked up at the pipes that emptied into the chamber. There were dozens to choose from.

He picked one at random—a big one just overhead. Kitster and Dorn boosted him up and handed him his tool bag.

Anakin took out his beamdrill. There was not much power left, but he had a feeling that he'd need it. The beamdrill could cut through just about anything: rock, duracrete—even armor plate.

All Anakin needed to do was find a drainpipe that led up into an empty room, and then cut his way out.

He inched through the pipe. There was hardly any sand here. Wherever this pipe led, it had not been used in a long time.

Perfect, he thought. He imagined a safe, abandoned warehouse.

He inched along, clunking as he pushed with his toes and shoved his tool bag ahead. The pipe took him up to a Y-shaped intersection. He looked up the left end, and then the right.

He didn't know which way to go. He turned off his glow rod to see if he could spot light in either direction. If he could see light, then it would mean that the tunnel came to an end nearby.

No sooner had he powered down the glow rod than he heard growling from the pipe on his right. He'd heard that same sound before at Watto's junkyard: *womp rats!*

The dirty rodents often burrowed beneath big sheets of metal. A full-grown womp rat could be as long as a man. They were big enough to carry off children and even full-grown Jawas.

Anakin didn't have a blaster, and he doubted that a womp rat would be scared of his teeth.

All he had was his beamdrill.

Anakin fumbled with its controls in the dark. He set the plasma beam for a long, narrow ray.

The womp rats stalked closer. He could hear their feet pounding the metal pipe. Anakin screamed, hoping they would back off.

For a fraction of a second, it worked.

He swung the nozzle of the breamdrill up, just as a womp rat charged. He pulled the trigger on the beam actuator. A searing white stream of superheated gas sprayed from the beamdrill. It acted like a flame thrower.

Up the tunnel the womp rat's fierce red eyes reflected the beam's light. It growled and bared its enormous incisors, just as the beamdrill sliced through it!

Behind, other womp rats snarled and backed away. Anakin scampered into the left fork of the tunnel, eager to escape.

Anakin followed the pipe. A dozen times it twisted and met smaller pipes.

Each time it did, he carefully took the handle of his glow rod and scratched an X into the roof overhead. That way he'd know how to get back.

Finally he reached a juncture and saw a drainpipe straight overhead. Anakin turned off his glow rod, then sat beneath the pipe for a second, listening. The room overhead seemed quiet. He squeezed into the pipe, climbing up until he neared the drain. The drain cover was secured with rusted bolts.

Anakin considered cutting through them. They looked so flimsy, he decided that if he just hit them, they'd probably snap. He banged against the drain cover with the handle of his glow rod.

A bolt broke with a *clank*. Suddenly he heard a door *whoosh* open.

Someone whispered in Huttese, "Did you hear that?" The voice sounded mechanical, like a droid's vocoder.

"What?" a similar voice asked.

"There's someone in here!"

Anakin held still, not daring to move.

A light snapped on. Two figures crept into the room. He could see them through the grate. They were Morseerians—creatures with green skin, long lumpy heads, and four arms. Since Morseerians breathe methane, they both wore goggles and gas masks. The speakers on the masks made their voices sound mechanical.

Anakin recognized the two immediately. They were space pirates. These Morseerians sometimes came to Watto's junkyard looking for spare parts. The large enclosure overhead was some kind of storage room that had once housed some heavy cleaning equipment.

The pirates began searching the room, shining strong beam lights into the corners. Anakin slid down the pipe, trying not to make any noise.

"Hey," one pirate said. "Look at that drain cover. Someone's been working at it."

Desperately, Anakin dropped down the pipe until he reached the main junction. Overhead, the light flashed around as the pirates neared.

His feet touched the ground, and Anakin slithered to safety just as a wrenching noise came from above. Rust and dirt drifted through a strong beam of light.

Anakin hid. He hardly dared to breathe. The Morseerians were as big as humans, but with larger heads and shoulders. They couldn't crawl down the pipe.

"Think someone has been trying to break in here?" one of the Morseerians asked.

The pirates seemed mighty suspicious. Anakin had a brilliant idea.

He tried to remember exactly how the womp rat had growled.

He felt back, low in his throat, and made a similar noise. To Anakin it sounded like the king of all womp rats, crying out for blood!

For heart-pounding seconds, he waited for the pirate's reactions.

"What's that?" a pirate asked. "A sick worrt?"

"Nah, dirty womp rat vermin," the other pirate grumbled. Suddenly a blinding blue light flashed in front of Anakin's eyes. A sizzling blaster bolt slammed into the pipe. Shards of hot metal and bits of rust flew.

Anakin tried to blink the dirt from his eyes. His heart raced. That blaster bolt had been close!

"Think you got him?" a pirate asked.

"Doubt it," the other Morseerian said. "But I'll bet he doesn't come around here again. Better check the money chest, just to make sure."

Anakin hardly dared to breathe. Overhead he heard clanking, the squeaking of hinges, and the sudden rattle as someone picked up a handful of coins.

"Looks good to me," one of the pirates said.

The pirates put the grate back on. Then they used their booted feet to stomp it snugly into place.

Anakin rubbed at his eyes. They were full of grit. He wanted to get out of there fast.

But something held him back: *pirate treasure*.

Anakin was honest, but he needed money desperately. Jira had already contacted the smugglers, and they would be here within the hour to take the Ghostling children home. First they would demand money.

Now Anakin had stumbled upon some.

He couldn't leave without it.

CHAPTER NINE

Anakin waited several moments. As stealthily as he could, he wriggled back up the pipe until he reached the drain cover. Sweat poured off of him. Climbing the pipe quietly was hard work.

He pushed the cover gently. It came off. The Morseerian pirates had actually broken the bolts for him! Anakin felt tempted to leave a thank you note after he took their money.

He carefully lifted the heavy iron cover, then slid it across the floor.

In seconds, he entered the storage room.

There was no light. He flipped on his glow rod and looked around. Old crates, most of them covered in dust, filled the room.

An old air cooler was built into a niche over the door, but it didn't work. The room felt stiflingly hot.

Anakin looked on the floor. It, too, was covered dust. No one had cleaned it for decades.

It wasn't hard to figure out where the pirates hid the treasure box. Anakin simply followed their foot-prints in the dust.

Anakin's heart pounded. He gripped his beamdrill as if it were a blaster, afraid that the pirates would come back at any moment. He tried not to imagine what they'd do if they caught him.

He reached some boxes covered with a tarp. He gently lifted it. Beneath the tarp was a locked freight box.

The treasure!

He tried to lift the box. It was so heavy he doubted that even a hulking Whiphid could have budged it.

Anakin didn't have a key for the lock.

But he did have a beamdrill.

He adjusted the drill settings so that it would give off a small, narrow beam of plasma. He flipped it on. The drill hissed like a snake, and emitted a steady blue tongue of flame.

He set the beam into the lock and began to cut through. The metal turned red and molten, dripping into a puddle on the floor. Anakin was an expert with a beamdrill. He had to cut apart bits of old spaceships all the time.

But this was the first time he'd ever cut into a freight box.

In seconds, he flipped open the lid. Inside the box was a fortune in coins from a hundred worlds!

Here on Tatooine, people used hard currency. Anakin knew the worth of many of the pieces. He grabbed the most valuable coins and shoved them into the deep pockets of his Jawa robe.

They clinked softly, music to his ears.

Anakin quickly counted a good three thousand wupiupi worth of coins.

But he hadn't counted on how keen the ears of the Morseerian pirates might be! He heard a scuffling and managed to flip off the power to his glow rod just before the door whisked open. He dodged behind the dusty crates. The Morseerians flashed their beam lights over the room.

"Look," a pirate said. "The grate's off the floor. Someone is in here!"

Anakin stifled the urge to scream. *The pirates had blasters. They wouldn't hesitate to shoot!*

CHAPTER TEN

The pirates stood in the doorway. Anakin hid behind the crates, fumbling once again with the settings on his beamdrill.

He set it to maximum length, wide beam. He could tell the drill's power was almost gone. At these settings, the power would run out almost instantly.

When the light beams were trained on the far side of the room, Anakin rose up in the darkness. He aimed his beamdrill and pulled the trigger.

The beams flooded the room with light. The Morseerians screamed. They were terrified of the rays. The pirates breathed methane. If the beam hit their breather masks, the whole building would blow up like a bomb!

Anakin hadn't counted on the fact that the pirates had four arms. Each pirate had a beam light, but also held two blasters.

Both pirates opened fire as they retreated out the door. Green blaster bolts sizzled through the air, blowing crates into pieces of flying debris, tearing through the walls, burning past Anakin's feet.

Anakin screamed and rushed at the pirates, even as they backed out the door, fleeing in panic.

He kept the flame shooting at the door as he raced for the sewer drain. The beamdrill suddenly sputtered empty. He hurled the drill through the doorway and dove headfirst down the drain.

After nearly crushing his head, Anakin reached the bottom of the pipe and jackknifed back along the pipe he'd come through.

Above him, he could hear the pirates curse. They rushed to the pipe and began shooting down into it, but they were too late

"Better get a new lock," Anakin shouted as he crawled to safety.

Later, scrambling down the pipe, Anakin wondered how soon the slave hunters might come after him and his friends.

He only knew that he had to find a way out of the pipes. Then he could go back and get the others.

He reached a juncture, turned again, and found an old drainpipe. He climbed up and reached the drain cover.

The pipe opened into a warehouse, where food crates were stacked all around. Lights were on.

He could only be in one place: The storage room for the Mos Espa Galactic Food Emporium—just down the street from Watto's junkyard!

Anakin climbed up to the drain cover and pushed. Its bolts looked old and rusted, but he couldn't get the leverage he needed.

He tried banging with the handle of his glow rod, hoping that it wouldn't break before the bolts did.

A voice overhead demanded, "What are you doing?"

A huge man peered through the drain cover.

"Drain inspector," Anakin said, coming up with the first lie that sprang to his lips. "Could you give me a hand with this?"

The big man stared down at him, unbelieving. "Escaped slave is more like it," he said, "I should call store security." He glanced toward a nearby door.

Anakin swallowed back his fear. "Please don't."

He couldn't see the man well through the drain screen. He was just a rough outline. But slowly Anakin began to see details of his clothes. The man wore a simple tunic made of cheap fabric, as dull as the sands of Tatooine. There was a familiar look to his face. He was weathered, beaten down by life. Anakin had seen that look a thousand times, on the faces of other slaves.

"Please," Anakin said. "Help us!"

The fellow licked his lips and looked again nervously at the door.

"Go away," the slave begged. "I have a family to protect."

"First pull off the grate."

"You'll get us all killed," the man objected.

"Pull off the grate and walk away. Don't come back for a while," Anakin said. "No one will ever know."

The fellow looked around nervously. Sweat broke on his brow.

"Please," Anakin said. "They're just children I'm trying to save. All of them are kids."

The man reached down and yanked the drain cover. Metal twisted as it broke from the floor. Only then did Anakin realize how big the slave was. He was a strong man, with massive arms made hard by long hours of lifting and stacking crates. Anakin could never have removed the drain cover without his help.

"You've got twenty minutes," the slave said as he walked out of the storage room and turned off the lights.

Anakin raced back to his friends. He had to get them out of the pipes while the warehouse grate was still open.

He passed junction after junction. All the pipes looked exactly the same. At each junction he paused for half a second just to make sure he was still heading the right way.

Once he passed a turn and thought he was lost. He'd marked it, but not clearly enough. He stopped and gouged out a clearer mark.

He'd nearly reached the big chamber when he saw a light ahead. Someone was scrambling toward him.

He saw Arawynne with a glow rod. Behind her he could hear heavy breathing, the grunts and cries of Ghostling children.

"Anakin, quick!" she cried. "Turn around."

"What's wrong?" he asked.

"Slave hunters!" Arawynne shouted. "They're in the pipes, following us!"

Anakin couldn't turn around. There wasn't enough room. Instead he scurried backward until he reached a juncture.

Arawynne's expression was grim, and Anakin realized that something horrible had happened.

"What else is wrong?" he asked.

"Coniel, the boy you pulled from the sand, is unconscious. Dorn has him. Dorn's trying to catch up, but he can't move very fast, carrying a child. He said he'll try to meet us at Bantha Rock."

Bantha Rock. That was where the smuggler ship was supposed to land.

"Anakin, I'm scared," Arawynne confessed. "I don't think Dorn's following us anymore. I think he knows he'll get caught, so he's trying to lead the slave catchers away from us."

That sounded like something Dorn would do.

Just then, there was a distant *thwing,* the sound of blaster fire, followed shortly by more.

Anakin felt himself get cold all over. He was "worried about Dorn, more worried than he'd ever been in his life. But worrying wouldn't do any good.

Dorn was gone.

Anakin raced back until he reached the juncture, then turned and led the children up to the storeroom at the market.

He opened the back door of the market and looked out.

He'd been in the drainage system for a long time. Night had begun to fall on Tatooine. The shadows were deep and thick. He hoped that it wasn't too late to reach the smuggler's ship.

At this point, readers who chose to follow the adventure in the *Star Wars* Adventures Game Book can return to the novel *Trouble on Tatooine*.

CHAPTER ELEVEN

Anakin raced to the junkyard. Luckily, Watto was away on unexpected, last-minute business—and hadn't taken his landspeeder. It was a beat-up old thing, but Anakin had made sure that there wasn't a faster speeder on Tatooine.

He whipped it through the darkening streets, around to the back of the Mos Espa Galactic Food Emporium.

Jawas and scurriers were pawing through the garbage behind the market. They hardly paid any attention as Pala, Kitster, Arawynne, and the Ghostling children ran out of the shadows and jumped into the back of the landspeeder.

Anakin threw dirty old blankets over them, ones that he normally used to keep the sun off of Watto's junk.

He hit the thrusters.

Just as he sped out of the alley, the back door of the market burst open. A pair of slave hunters stood there: fierce Rodians with heavy blasters.

They let loose a salvo of blaster fire. A bolt ripped through the housing on the rear of the landspeeder as Anakin whipped around the corner.

Anakin realized dully that Watto would probably never even notice another hole in his speeder. He shot through the streets of Mos Espa, hit the open desert, and tightened down on the throttle.

The landspeeder hummed, singing over the sand. It bounced with every rise and fall of the dunes. The stars tonight shone fiercely bright.

He whisked over the desert sands with his light off. The landspeeder screamed past a pair of Tusken Raiders who rode upon a lone bantha.

Soon he neared Bantha Rock, a huge red stone that thrust out of the ground out in the canyons. In the darkness, the rock looked more like a giant bantha than ever.

Anakin watched overhead, looking between stars for the lights of ships. Distantly, he saw the blinking landing lights of huge freighters and other ships that dove toward Mos Espa spaceport.

But he didn't see any ships nearby. No ships landing, nothing taking off. He supposed that that was a good sign. Maybe the smugglers were waiting for him.

Or maybe they never came in the first place.

He powered up the lights on the landspeeder. They cut through the darkness like lightning in a summer dust storm.

Ahead, he spotted an old woman beside a clump of rocks. Jira stood up and waved.

Pala climbed from under the tarp and looked around. Jira sat all alone on the pile of rocks. Pala couldn't see any sign of a smuggler's ship.

"Are they here yet?" Pala asked.

Jira shook her head. "They only come when I signal that we're ready. And we have a problem: I couldn't get enough money."

Pala's heart fell. She'd gone through all the trouble to get the Ghostling children free. She'd been captured and nearly killed. But for what?

Dorn was gone, one of her oldest friends, along with a Ghostling child.

"I have some money!" Anakin shouted. Pala couldn't imagine Annie having anywhere near enough. But suddenly he reached in his pockets and began pulling out coins from a dozen worlds.

"Annie," Jira asked, "where did you get this?"

"Uh, I sort of found it in the pipes."

Jira took a handful of coins and looked at them closely.

"Will it be okay?" Pala asked.

"Smugglers aren't particular," Jira said. "Yes, it will be okay. There's more than enough."

Words could not express how astonished Pala was at the sight of Anakin's money, or how relieved she felt. She ran to him and gave him a hug. Now she would be free...if the smugglers showed up.

The other children all crawled out from beneath the blankets and stood on the warm desert sands. The Ghostlings still glowed with their own special light. Even bedraggled and dirty, they were beautiful. But Kitster looked miserable. He stood hunched over, worrying about Dorn.

Jira went to the rock and picked up a little glow rod. She raised it high overhead and powered it on, then swung it in a slow circle. She turned it off, for a second, then repeated the movement twice more.

When she finished, the thrusters of a spaceship became visible, high atop Bantha Rock. Blue flames erupted from its exhaust ports, and the ship rose up from a jumble of rocks, where it had been hidden from the naked eye.

For a moment it soared into the air, looking for all the world like a shooting star. Then it veered back toward them, a battered Corellian freighter diving in for a landing.

Only when the ship had touched down and the hatch had swung open did Pala begin to realize that she was going to make it out of this alive.

Pala hugged Anakin again and broke into tears of relief and sadness—relief that she was going to live, sadness because she knew that she'd never see Anakin again.

A huge man rushed from the hatch of the freighter and stood on the gangplank, a man with long dark hair that flowed over his shoulders. The red loading lights in the hatch cast an eerie glow over him. He wore a pair of heavy blasters—one strapped to each leg.

He looked at Jira and the children. He shook his head in wonder. "Do you have the money?"

Pala had expected his voice to be hard, for he had the look of a hardened criminal. But instead it was soft, almost kind.

"Yes," Jira said. She took a bag of coins, the scrapings from every slave in Mos Espa, and handed it to him. The smuggler didn't look in the bag. He merely hefted it thoughtfully.

"It will do," he said. He counted the children. "I can squeeze them all on board—barely."

CHAPTER TWELVE

Kitster and Anakin looked at each other in surprise. Neither one of them had planned to leave Tatooine. It would have been too much to hope, but now the smuggler was offering to take them away.

"Uh," Anakin said quickly. "I'm not going."

"Not going?" the smuggler asked.

"My mother's here," Anakin said. "I can't leave her."

"Are you sure?" the smuggler asked. "Chances like this don't come by more than once in a lifetime."

Anakin squinted at the smuggler. For a moment, he looked as if he was listening to a distant voice. "Yes they do," he said finally. "I hope."

He seemed firm in his choice. He really did believe that someday he'd get free. But Kitster knew that a chance like this might never come again for either of them.

Kitster went to his best friend and stood looking at him for a moment. "Wow," he said, still so much in shock that he couldn't believe his luck. "I guess this is good-bye."

"Yeah," Anakin said. Anakin gave him a hug, and Kitster squeezed him hard. He felt Anakin try to hold all the pain inside.

It didn't feel right to Kitster, leaving like this. Dorn was gone, and Kitster would be taking his place. In doing so, he'd leave Anakin more alone than ever. "All your friends will be gone," Kitster said.

"I'll still have Wald and Amee," Anakin said. That was true, but it wasn't the same. Anakin played with the younger kids, but he'd practically been raised with Pala, Kitster, and Dorn. They weren't just friends anymore. They were brothers and sisters.

"Yeah, you'll always have friends," Kitster said. Pala and the Ghostlings were saying good-bye to Jira. The old woman wept with relief to see them go, and Kitster gave her a hug too.

Jira mussed up Kitster's hair and said, "I'm glad you'll be free, even though I'll miss you."

He thought of all the good times he'd had with her, and said, "I'm glad I'll be free, even though I'll miss *you*."

Anakin warned the smuggler, "Sir, my friends have transmitters in them, and slave trackers."

"Don't worry," the smuggler said. "I know how to handle that."

Kitster turned and staggered toward the space-ship. Pala and the Ghostlings went inside.

As he drew near, he stared at the big smuggler under the red loading lights. There was something familiar about him, something strange. It was almost as if Kitster had met him in a dream.

Kitster stumbled closer, not believing his eyes. The smuggler was older than he remembered, and he'd cut off his beard and grown his hair. But Kitster recognized the face and the deep soft voice.

It wasn't until Kitster reached the hatchway that he had a strange sense of who the man was. He recognized the ragged white scar that ran from the joint of his thumb up to the middle of his wrist. He still wore a golden bracelet, like a slave's manacle.

Kitster stopped on the gangplank, reached up and touched the golden bracelet. Kitster's throat tightened, and tears flooded into his eyes. He couldn't speak.

"You like the bracelet?" his father asked. "I keep it as a reminder. I was a slave once, too."

Kitster was about to speak, to say the first words he'd spoken to his father since he was kidnapped by the slavers all those years ago, when suddenly his father snapped back, raised a blaster, and shoved him toward the hatch.

A landspeeder was coming, shooting fast over the desert, with its headlights off.

"Get inside," his father shouted. "It's a trap!"

CHAPTER THIRTEEN

The landspeeder screamed out of the darkness and out of the night, slamming to a halt just beneath the hatch.

The smuggler held his heavy blaster in his right hand and took aim at the driver. Almost too late, Kitster recognized what was happening. He jumped from the hatch and knocked the blaster just as his father fired.

The shots went wide, blowing holes in the ground.

From the darkened landspeeder, Dorn's cheerful voice shouted, "Hey, hold your fire!"

He leaped out of the landspeeder, reached into the back seat, and pulled out the Ghostling child. The small boy, not more than three, looked around with wide eyes. He'd regained consciousness. "I'm sorry I'm late," Dorn said, "but I had to lose those slave hunters."

"Dorn!" Anakin shouted in glee. He and Jira ran to Dorn, hugged him, and ushered him up to the smuggler's ship.

Rakir Banai stopped them as they were about to enter. "I don't have room for all of you," he said. "I'm overloaded as it is."

"Is this about money?" Jira asked. "We have a bit more."

"It's not about money," Kitster's dad said. "The life-support systems just can't handle it. Someone has to stay behind."

The look of panic on Dorn's face was frightening. Everyone in Mos Espa knew that he'd helped free the Ghostling children. He wouldn't last a week.

The child in his arms began to cry, fearing that he'd be left behind. Numbly, Dorn set the boy down on the gangplank, and let him run inside.

Kitster knew what he had to do.

He had to let Dorn take his place.

No one had recognized Kitster when he was caught. The chances were good that no one would be looking for him.

"Go ahead," Kitster told Dorn. "You take my seat."

"Thanks," Dorn said. He embraced Kitster gratefully and ran into the ship.

Kitster looked up at the man he thought was his father. Rakir Banai gazed down on him, put a hand on his shoulder. "You're a brave boy. You're going to go far."

For just a second, Kitster was tempted to reveal the one secret he'd held all his life. He was tempted to ask, "My name is Kitster—do you know who I am?"

But he knew that if he said those words, his father wouldn't leave Tatooine without him. If he spoke those words, his father would leave Dorn or Pala or one of the Ghostling children here instead.

"Thank you, sir," Kitster said to his father. "I hope to meet you again one day."

He walked down the gangplank, back toward Anakin and Tatooine and a life of slavery and uncertainty. He kept his secret in his heart.

For Kitster, it was not a hard thing to do. He'd lived this way for too long.

CHAPTER FOURTEEN

Sebulba glided through the desert on a land-speeder with Djas Puhr and Gondry close behind.

Ahead of him, a pair of seeker droids hummed across the desert at top speed. Silently, Sebulba cursed. He wished that the droids would move faster.

These slaves had beaten him for the last time. Gardulla had planned an elaborate execution, complete with Dorn and the largest flesh-eating creature he could find. He'd planned to have a blind-folded Gamorrean shoot at Ghostling children while they were trapped in a pen.

But once again, the slaves had escaped Sebulba, made him look bad, and cost him a fortune.

He was determined to wipe them out.

This time, there would be no losing track of the slaves. His seeker droids had the scents and skin samples from Pala and Dorn in their files. Even if the seekers were destroyed, backup files were stored elsewhere. The slaves wouldn't be able to hide for long.

The seekers whipped over the desert, dipping and bobbing as they bounced over the dunes. They headed straight for Bantha Rock.

Sebulba glared ahead, and silently wished that they would pick up speed.

Suddenly, ahead, he saw a bright light lift into the sky from the base of Bantha Rock. It was pushing the dull shape of a Corellian freighter, its running lights off.

"Looks like we're late again," Djas Puhr said.

The spaceship engaged its thrusters and shot into the night like a flaming star. In seconds it was gone.

When Sebulba reached the base of Bantha Rock, he found no slaves, only a landspeeder. It was Jabba's landspeeder, the same one that Dorn had driven into Mos Espa earlier in the day. Its thrusters were turned off, along with its repulsor-lift, so that it lay dead on the sand, making pinging sounds as its engines cooled in the night air.

The seeker droids both halted a few meters from the landspeeder and made the same report. "Sir, the scent trail ends here. The slaves have escaped!"

Gone. All the slaves were gone—Dorn, Pala, the Ghostling children, and their accomplices.

Rage twisted in Sebulba's gut. His eyes burned with fury. He pulled out his blaster and filled Jabba's landspeeder full of holes.

Soon the landspeeder was just a burning hunk of wreckage. He left it for the Jawas to scavenge.

On a distant plateau, Anakin and Jira watched Sebulba's fireworks display. They couldn't hear the curses he muttered, but they knew they had him beat.

They laughed and cheered, while Kitster sat silently in the back of the landspeeder, huddled in a ball. He looked miserable.

"We beat them, Kitster," Anakin said. "You don't have to be afraid anymore. Did you hear me?"

"Yeah," Kitster said.

Anakin stared at his friend and tried to figure out his mood.

Kitster glanced up at him and said in a reassuring tone, "It's good. I'm all right, Annie."

"You sure?" Anakin asked.

Kitster nodded. "Positive."

Anakin couldn't figure out why Kitster was in such a quiet mood. Maybe he was just tired. They'd both worked so hard the past few days. Anakin felt all of his muscles loosening, the stress seeping out of him. He thought he'd be able to sleep like a runkit for the next month.

Maybe Kitster is sad, Anakin thought. *We beat Sebulba, but in doing so we've lost two of our best friends.*

"Don't be sad," Anakin said. "We'll see them again someday. I promise."

Kitster looked up at him and smiled weakly. "You always keep your promises, don't you, Annie?"

"Yeah, I do."

They climbed into the landspeeder. Anakin drove. The night wind washed over his face, and he hurtled under the starlight. The desert had cooled. Scurriers leaped across the sand to get out of his path. It was pleasant, peaceful.

Jira said, "Anakin, Kitster, we have a few coins left over. I want you to have them."

"Us?" Kitster asked. "But that money belongs to the slaves."

"They gave the money to you children, to help you buy your freedom," Jira said. "I think you should keep it, and spend it wisely."

"How much is there?" Kitster asked.

"Almost a thousand."

Kitster whistled. "That's a lot. Annie, what will you do with all that money?"

Anakin thought about it. Five hundred wasn't nearly enough to buy freedom for himself or his mother. But Watto had been having him race a lot lately. If Anakin could win a couple of Podraces, he'd make lots of money. Eventually he could even earn his freedom.

Anakin drove Jira home and then dropped Kitster off for the night. When he got to the house, he looked through the window first. His mother was up late working again.

Her friend Matta was still sick, and her cruel master, Dengula, had threatened to send her to the spice mines if she didn't keep up with her quota on droid repairs.

So Shmi Skywalker was up working late for the third night in a row. She'd always said that the biggest problem in the universe was that no one helps anyone else. Now she was finding a way to help.

Anakin looked at his mom through the window and realized that she was like a sculptor, carving on a huge stone. In her own way, day after day, Shmi Skywalker made the biggest problem in the universe a little smaller. She just kept chipping away at it.

As he walked into the door, his mother looked up at him and set down her repair tools. She was shaking, her eyes were red from crying.

"Annie," she said. "I was so worried about you."

Anakin nodded. "It's all right. They're gone. They're safe."

She hurried out from behind her little worktable and gave him a hug.

"How's Matta?" Anakin asked.

"She's almost better. She'll be back to work tomorrow."

"I can help you with those droids," Anakin offered. His mother couldn't fix a droid half as fast as Anakin could.

"Oh, no you don't," his mother laughed. "I don't want you to do a thing, dirty as you are."

She peeled off the Jawa robe and threw it into the trash, then sent Anakin to clean up.

Two days later, Mos Espa was gearing up for a big race. Once again, Anakin faced Sebulba.

This time it was on the Podracer track.

He'd been round the course twice as he headed for his final run. Ahead of him, Sebulba's split-X screamed over the desert. Anakin fought Sebulba and Rimkar for the lead.

The twin suns of Tatooine glared on the flats, and a watery sheen rose off the white sands.

Anakin had just passed through the stadium, hearing the blaring voices of the announcers. The crowds had cheered.

Somewhere in the arena, his mother would be standing, perhaps biting her knuckles as she worried. Somewhere Kitster would be leaping up and down, cheering Anakin on.

We're all like trees in Gardulla's pleasure garden, Anakin thought, *trapped here, rooted in a place that we don't want to be.*

He thought about the strange little box in the cubbyhole above his bed. He thought about the dream that told him that he had to open the box from the *inside.* Maybe the dream wasn't talking about that old box at all. Maybe the dream had been telling him to look for a way to escape from Tatooine.

Maybe that's what I'm doing right now, Anakin thought.

Anakin drove by instinct. At times he seemed to fuse with his Podracer, become one with it, or maybe became more than either a man or a machine alone.

Now was one of those times.

He soared over the desert toward Metta Drop. When he hit it, his stomach always went out from under him, and he felt kind of sick. The best way to keep from getting sick, he'd discovered, was simply not to think about it, to fix his mind on something else.

At times like this, when his Podracer soared over the desert, Anakin felt as close as he could to being free.

He sailed over Metta Drop, and the Podracer fell away beneath him. He thought briefly about Pala, Dorn, Arawynne, and the Ghostling children.

By now, the Ghostlings would be home, joyfully reunited with their parents. He tried to imagine how happy they would be.

By now, the kidnapped children had all returned home. The future looked bright. The Ghostlings wouldn't die in Gardulla's pleasure garden for her amusement. Their mothers and fathers wouldn't have to spend long years grieving the loss.

Anakin couldn't imagine the joy they must feel. He'd never been to Datar. He'd never seen the hanging nests in the bayah trees that Ghostling children slept in. He'd never tasted the night air beneath Datar's silver moons, or watched a blaze bug light the heart of a trumpet flower as he struggled to keep awake.

Anakin imagined the Ghostling children sleeping peacefully in their mother's arms, with their brief captivity on Tatooine fading from memory like a bad dream.

He imagined where Dorn might be, or Pala, and how they must feel right now. Both of them would be heading home and places that they only dimly remembered, to blessed reunions with parents and family who would be strangers. He imagined them high above Tatooine, flying to a new home, soaring free.

What would it be like to be free?

He hit the bottom of Metta Drop. Suddenly Sebulba's Podracer swerved in front of him. The cruel Dug flashed his vents. The engine exhaust slammed Anakin's Podracer and sent him fishtailing out of control. His Podracer began to spin.

Anakin had seen crashes like this a hundred times—Podracers screaming over the desert, out of control, slamming into one another or into rocks.

By instinct alone, Anakin cut the thrusters and tried to right his steering. That would save the Podracer engines, mostly. The heavy engines slammed into the sand, sent a wall of debris flying, and split off in two directions. Anakin's Pod hit the ground with a bone-wrenching crash. It veered first left, then right, then went rolling over the desert, splintering apart.

The cockpit bounced against the hardpan.

For a brief second, Anakin was flying above the desert of Tatooine, flying above the crowds and the horrors, flying away like Dorn and Pala.

For a brief second he felt the hot wind in his face. He opened his mouth for his first sweet taste of freedom.